50 STATES
IN EVERY VEHICLE

AMBER STEWART

ILLUSTRATED BY
CARLES BALLESTEROS

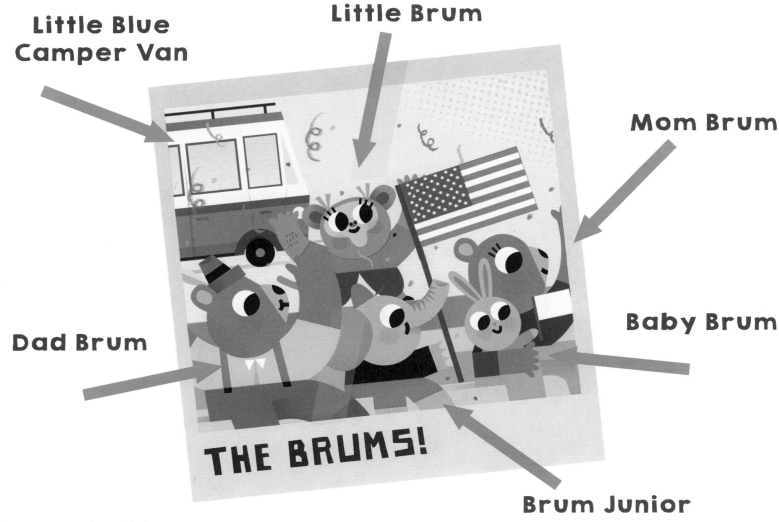

Little Blue Camper Van

Little Brum

Mom Brum

Dad Brum

Baby Brum

THE BRUMS!

Brum Junior

First American Edition 2018
Kane Miller, A Division of EDC Publishing

Copyright © 2018 Quarto Publishing plc
Published by arrangement with QED Publishing, an imprint of The Quarto Group.

For information contact:
Kane Miller, A Division of EDC Publishing
PO Box 470663
Tulsa, OK 74147-0663
www.kanemiller.com
www.edcpub.com
www.usbornebooksandmore.com

Library of Congress Control Number: 2017942231

Printed in China

2 3 4 5 6 7 8 9 10

ISBN: 978-1-61067-682-3

FSC
www.fsc.org

MIX
Paper from
responsible sources
FSC® C001701

50 STATES
IN EVERY VEHICLE

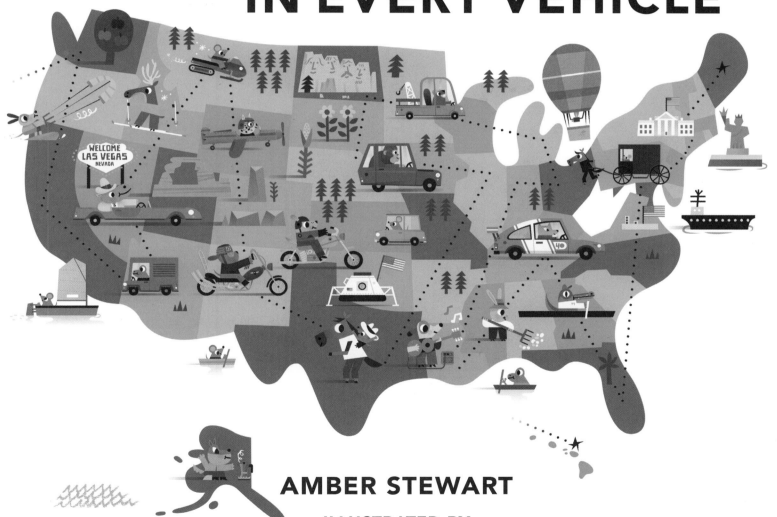

WELCOME
LAS VEGAS
NEVADA

AMBER STEWART

ILLUSTRATED BY
CARLES BALLESTEROS

Kane Miller
A DIVISION OF EDC PUBLISHING

The Brum family are off on a big adventure in their little blue camper van.

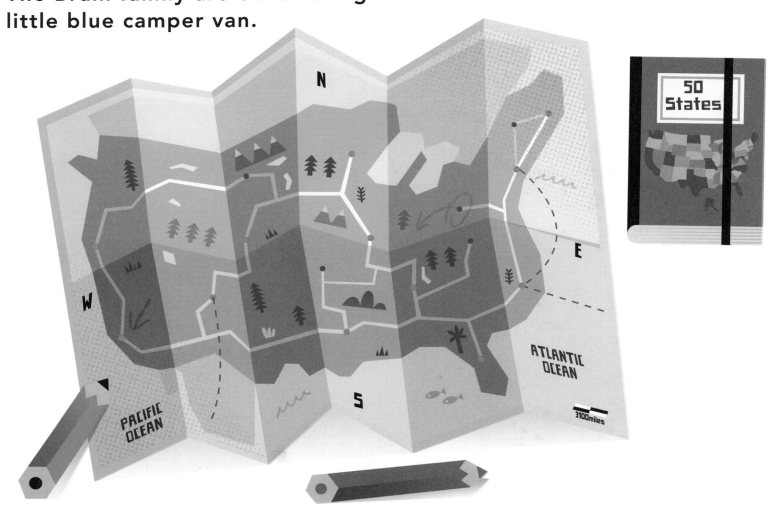

It's time to pack their things ...

They want to visit all fifty states!

"How many states have we done now?" asks Baby Brum as they drive along the interstate.

"Just one," says Mom Brum, "our home state of Maine."

SPEED
LIMIT
65

Baby Brum waves to the train puffing along the Conway Scenic Railroad in New Hampshire.

They drive under a Vermont covered bridge.
"Now you see us. Now you don't!"

They arrive in Massachusetts, and soon they are on the busy Boston streets.

Brum Junior is excited to see the planes at Logan International Airport.

Look at all the airplanes! There are two-seater planes, jumbo jets, planes waiting, planes taking off, and planes landing!

They are surprised it doesn't take long to drive through Rhode Island.

Did you know that Rhode Island is the smallest state? It's just 48 miles long and 37 miles wide.

How many states?

"State number five," says Mom Brum.

They make it to Connecticut in time to sail around the tall ships at the Mystic Seaport Museum.

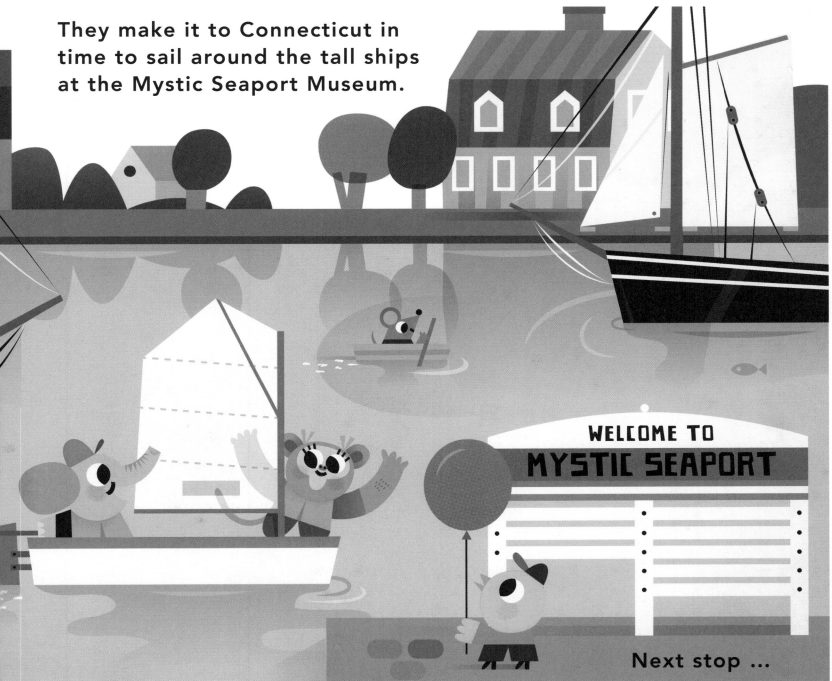

Next stop ...

"Car!" shouts Baby Brum, bouncing up and down as they hit the busy Manhattan streets. "Yellow car!"

"Taxi cab," says Mom Brum. "Lots of taxi cabs."

The next day, over a big New York breakfast, Mom and Dad Brum plan different routes.

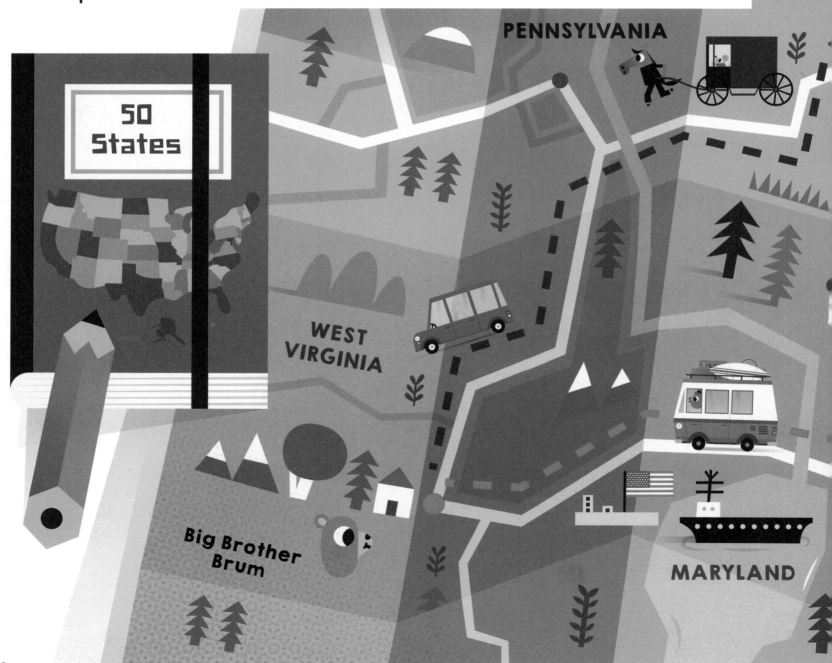

50 States

PENNSYLVANIA

WEST VIRGINIA

Big Brother Brum

MARYLAND

Dad Brum is going to drive to West Virginia to visit his big brother. On his way, he'll go through New Jersey, Delaware, and Maryland — there's so much to see!

Mom Brum and the little Brums are taking the train to see Niagara Falls by helicopter.

They'll then rent a car and drive through Pennsylvania on their way to West Virginia to meet Dad Brum.

Mom Brum drops off the rental car in West Virginia, and the little Brums tell Dad Brum all about their big adventure.

"Next stop is the president's house!" says Dad Brum as the little blue camper van chugs into Washington, D.C.

"How many states now?" asks Baby Brum.

"Let me see," says Mom Brum, counting, "I think this will be ..."

"Wait!" says Brum Junior. "Washington, D.C., is not a state. It is a district, and it's the capital of the United States!"

They tour the capital city in an open-top bus, seeing all of the sights. Then they drive through Virginia, watching the sun set over the hills as they make their way farther south.

Their trip south is a lot of fun, but they all like different things the best. Brum Junior likes North Carolina because he learns about the Wright Brothers' first flight near Kitty Hawk.

Mom Brum likes South Carolina because they get to pick and eat juicy peaches.

"Did you know," says Brum Junior, "the plane stayed in the air for a whole twelve seconds!"

Little Brum likes Georgia because she sees a huge truck, and the driver waves to her.

Florida is busy, busy, busy! It is one long roller-coaster ride of excitement from start to finish. The bustling Brum family sees rockets and rides and race cars.

Whoosh! Florida goes by in a rush of fun.

TO THE BEACH

Soon they are driving through the cotton fields in Alabama.

"Did you know," says Brum Junior, "the South is famous for growing cotton to make clothes."

Next, they drive through a forest and watch the loggers hard at work.

Before long they are in Mississippi.
They count the boats on the magnificent
Mississippi River and get ten.

The Brums' little blue camper van is dusty and squeaky. They have driven a long way by the time they arrive in New Orleans, Louisiana. Baby Brum isn't sure how many states they have visited.

We have driven through nineteen states, so Louisiana makes twenty!

"No wonder our van is squeaky," says Mom Brum. They take their van to a mechanic.

"Cars!" says Baby Brum.
"Cars are my business," says the mechanic.

The Brum family hops on a streetcar to get to their hotel in the French Quarter. Tomorrow they will pick up their non-squeaky van and continue on their grand tour!

The little blue van is fixed up and speedy.

Dad Brum wants to hurry through Arkansas and Tennessee to catch the Indy 500 race in Indiana. Mom Brum says, "Stop driving like an Indy driver! There are things to see along the way."

They take a Segway tour in Fort Smith, Arkansas.

They see fancy cars at the Lane Motor Museum in Nashville, Tennessee ...

... and they see famous horses in Louisville, Kentucky.

They make it to the racetrack in Indianapolis, Indiana, just in time to cheer their favorite driver to victory!

After all the hustle and bustle of race day, the Brum family enjoys the peace and quiet of a balloon flight in Ohio.

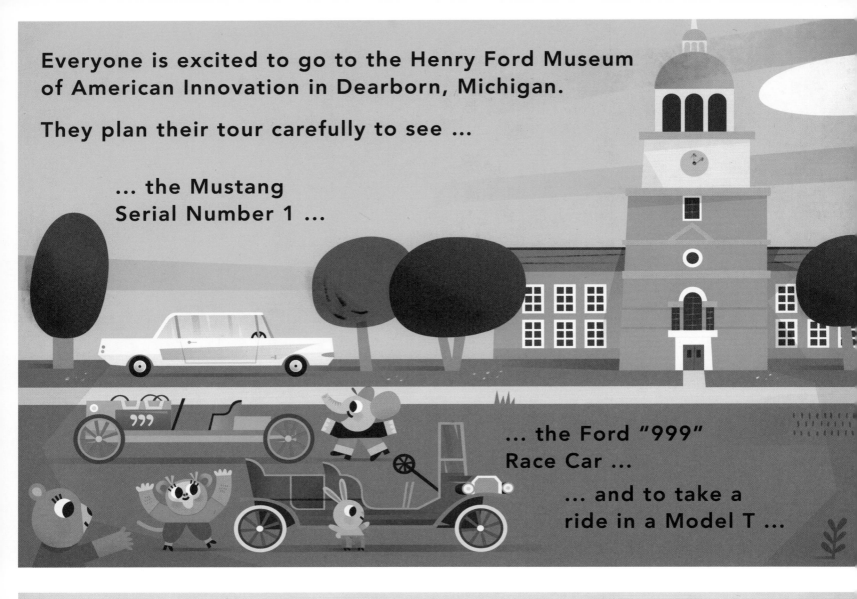

Everyone is excited to go to the Henry Ford Museum of American Innovation in Dearborn, Michigan.

They plan their tour carefully to see ...

... the Mustang Serial Number 1 ...

... the Ford "999" Race Car ...

... and to take a ride in a Model T ...

... before driving onto the ferry to take them across Lake Michigan to Wisconsin.

"Truck!" says Baby Brum happily. But Dad Brum isn't as happy to be stuck behind a Wisconsin logging truck.

The drive to Minnesota is long, hot, and dusty. The Brum family stop to have a picnic by a lake and take a pedal boat out.

They drive slowly through North Dakota and South Dakota, admiring the mountains and avoiding the cyclists whizzing by.

In Nebraska, the Brum family spends some time in a farming village. Brum Junior is excited to drive a little tractor, while Mom Brum and Dad Brum relax, sipping lemonade under a shady tree.

All too soon it's time to load up the van once more and head to Iowa.

They ride the steam train along the scenic old railroad in Boone County, puffing through valleys and under bridges.

Driving along Interstate 80, they see endless fields full of corn. Before they know it they have arrived in ...

INTERSTATE
80

... Chicago, Illinois.
"How many states now?" asks Baby Brum.

"Thirty-three!" says Little Brum.

"We're up high," says Baby Brum, as they ride the L train on their way to see a Chicago Cubs baseball game!

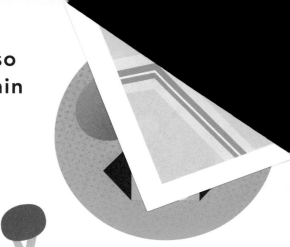

"Did you know," says Brum Junior, "we could also get to the game by bus, or even by bike! But train is the best way."

After the game, the Brum family packs up and gets ready to hit Route 66 for the next stage of their big adventure!

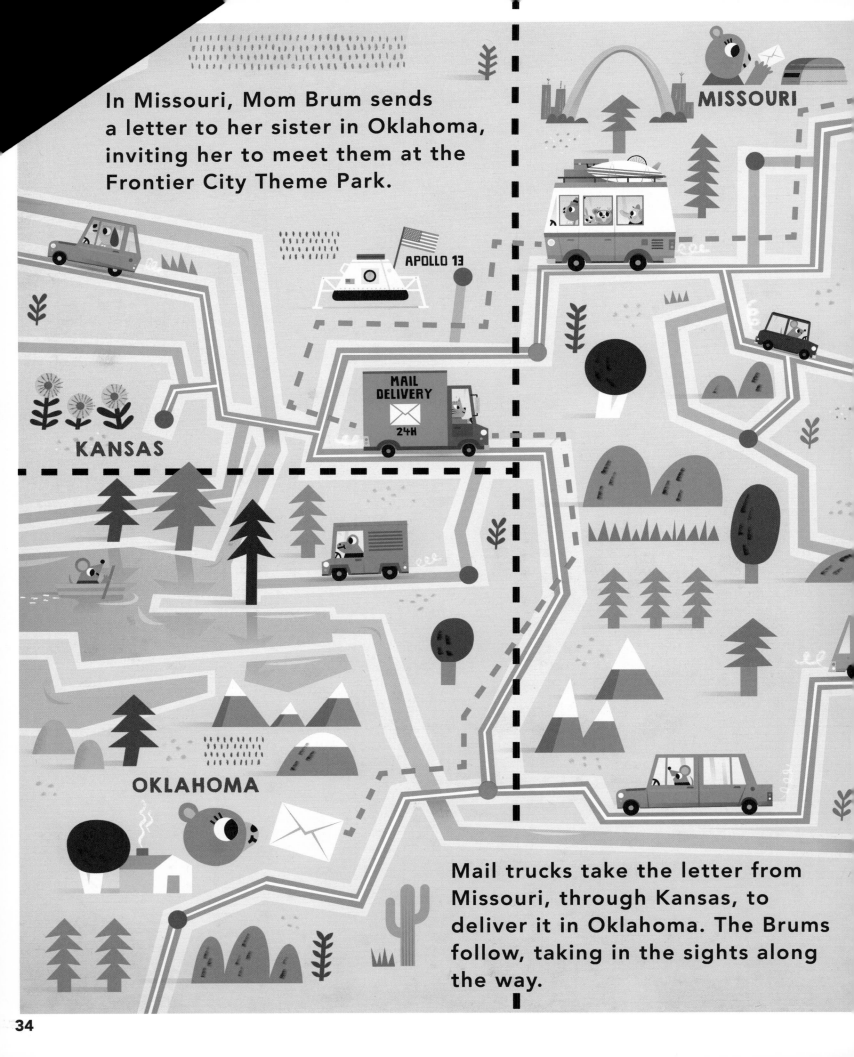

In Missouri, Mom Brum sends a letter to her sister in Oklahoma, inviting her to meet them at the Frontier City Theme Park.

APOLLO 13

MAIL DELIVERY 24H

MISSOURI

KANSAS

OKLAHOMA

Mail trucks take the letter from Missouri, through Kansas, to deliver it in Oklahoma. The Brums follow, taking in the sights along the way.

In Oklahoma City, Oklahoma, the two families meet for some fun at the fair!

WILD WEST WATER WORKS

SALOON

FRONTIER CITY

Did you know, the Pony Express was the fastest mail service in frontier times? It took just ten days to get mail from Missouri to California.

"Faster than our little blue van," says Dad Brum.

They make it to Texas, the last of the southern states on their trip.

It is full of things to see and do.

They see the fighter planes in Fort Worth. "I don't think you would see these at Logan," says Dad Brum.

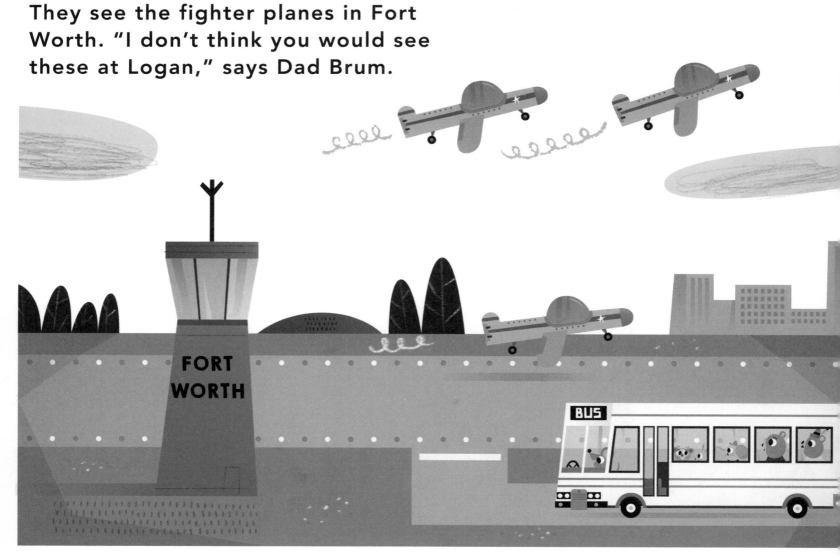

And they see more rockets and shuttles at Space Center Houston.

"Is the moon part of the fifty states?" asks Baby Brum.

"I wish!" says Brum Junior, who would love to fly to the moon one day.

What an amazing end to this part of the tour! Now it is time to leave Route 66.

In Albuquerque, New Mexico, they ride the cable car to the crestline of the Sandia Mountains and watch gleaming motorbikes speed past.

We're going up 4,000 feet in fifteen minutes!

SANDIA PEAK

SANDIA PEAK

Far down below they see mountains, volcano fields, and forests.

The Brums may not be the most athletic family, but they give everything a try, from riding sand cars in Colorado to white-water rafting in Wyoming.

SAND DUNES

WHITE WATER

Sitting around the campfire in Yellowstone National Park, they look at the pictures of their adventures and feel proud.

The weather in Montana is freezing! It's time to get their winter gear out of the van.

They have a great time skiing in Montana and Idaho.

Baby Brum is sad to pat the sleigh pony goodbye as they set off.

But he cheers up when he sees the red landscape of Utah. Red is Baby Brum's favorite color.

How many states now, Little Brum?

Forty-three!

"I miss the snow," says Little Brum. "Let's go to Alaska and see the polar bears and ride on an icebreaker."

"Next time," promises Mom Brum. Alaska is too far away for this trip, but the Brum family count Alaska as number forty-four.

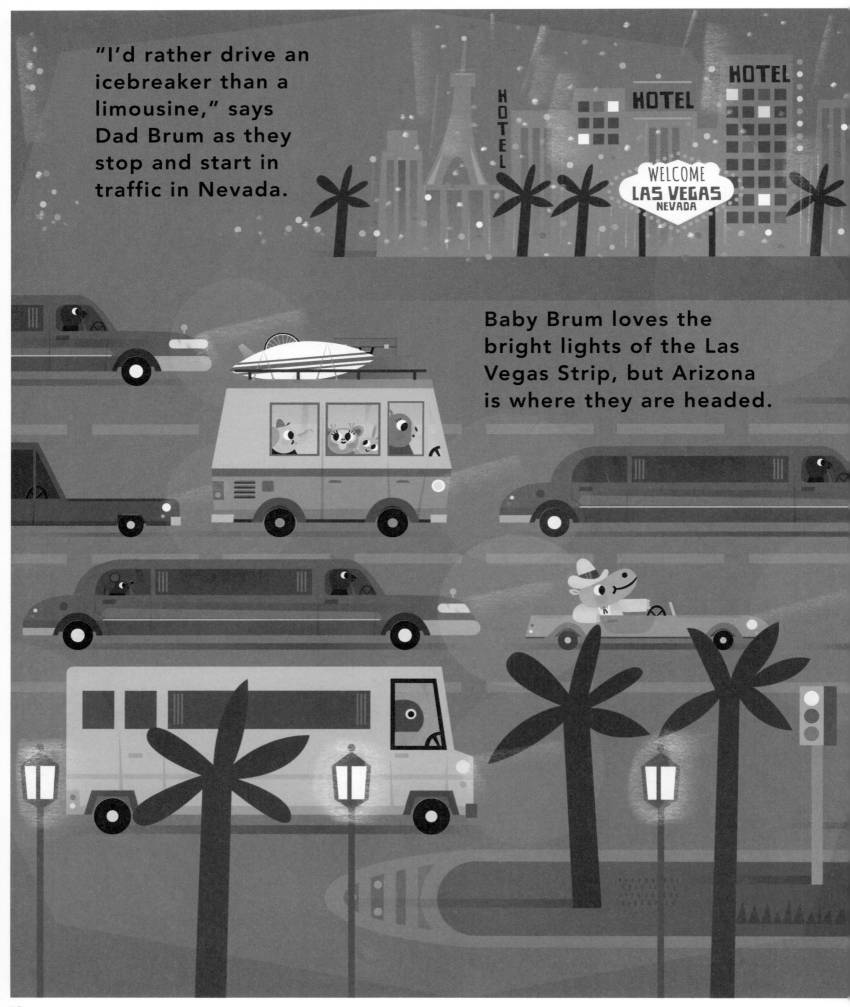

"I'd rather drive an icebreaker than a limousine," says Dad Brum as they stop and start in traffic in Nevada.

Baby Brum loves the bright lights of the Las Vegas Strip, but Arizona is where they are headed.

HOTEL

HOTEL

HOTEL

WELCOME
LAS VEGAS
NEVADA

The Brums take an airplane tour of the Grand Canyon.

Baby Brum waves to the people on the glass skywalk, but they are too busy looking down at the canyon, 2,000 feet below, to wave back.

"Never mind, Baby Brum, Arizona is state forty-six!" says Little Brum.

The sun is shining as they drive on the busy Pacific Coast Highway in California.

No one minds the traffic jam as they look at the sun on the water and see huge tankers moving slowly along the horizon.

Whir-er! Whir-er!

FIRE DEPARTMENT 33

Fire engines scream past, heading to a forest fire up in the hills.

In San Francisco, they ride their bikes over the Golden Gate Bridge and watch the sailboats race beneath them.

They take a cable car up a steep hill. Baby Brum waves to everyone they pass, and this time everyone waves back!

In Oregon, they take their bikes out again to ride on the Interstate 205 Bikeway.

Brum Junior is excited about everything there is to do.

"We could go out on a crabbing boat," he says.

"And in Oregon you can kite surf on rivers and on the ocean."

It is nearly the end of the trip!

The Brum family spends a day on their cousin's apple farm in Washington. Dad Brum has arranged for their cousin to have the little blue van to use on his farm.

They give it a good wash and say goodbye because now it's time to fly.

The family ends their trip in style with a beach trip to Hawaii.

EMERGENCY
EXIT

"State number fifty!"
they cheer.

HOTEL

BEACH
STOP

BEACH TOUR 850

Goodbye, Brum family,
see you next time!